Shikari Shambu
Based on an idea sent by Sanjay Pai, Bangalore
Illustrations: V. B. Halbe
LOOK AT THIS ADVERTISEMENT...
Baboon escaped en route to zoo! Believed to have entered forest. Finder will be given a reward of Rs. 2000/-. Contact Collector's office for more details.
WHERE ARE YOU GOING?
I'M OFF TO THE COLLECTOR'S OFFICE. I'M GOING AFTER THIS BABOON.
AT THE COLLECTOR'S OFFICE —
SHAMBU, WE'RE SO GLAD YOU'RE GOING AFTER THIS BABOON.
WELL, I'VE RESCUED LIONS AND TIGERS. THIS IS EASY.
WE'D BETTER FOLLOW SHAMBU WITH THE CAGE.
GOOD IDEA.
WELL, I'VE COME PRETTY DEEP INTO THE FOREST, AND THERE'S NO SIGN OF THE ANIMAL.
AFTER SEVERAL HOURS —
HERE'S A RUINED BUILDING... WHAT'S THAT DARTING INSIDE? SEEMED LIKE A BABOON...
CAREFUL NOW, SHAMBU, OLD CHAP.

IT'S QUITE DARK IN HERE...
SCARY!
SWOOSH
EEYOW!
I MUST GET AWAY.
MEANWHILE—
I THINK SHAMBU WENT INSIDE THIS BUILDING.
LOOK! THERE'S THE BABOON ON THE BALCONY!
I'LL LEAP FOR THAT BRANCH AND COME DOWN.

LOOK! THE BABOON'S ON THE GROUND. AFTER IT OR IT'LL GET AWAY!
NO, LOOK!
HELP! I'M FALLING!
OOPH!
DID YOU SEE SHAMBU'S LEAP?
YES, THAT WAS SPLENDID! BETTER THAN TARZAN!
THAT WAS A REMARKABLE FEAT, SHAMBU!
YES, YOU'VE REALLY EARNED THE REWARD!
OH! IT WAS NOTHING REALLY.

Shikari Shambu
Script: Iyer Prasad B.
Illustrations: V.B. Halbe
SAHIB! SAHIB! THERE ARE TWO MAN-EATERS RUNNING AMOK IN THE JUNGLE!
ONE OF THEM IS A TIGER AND THE OTHER A LEOPARD.
T...T... TWO MAN-EATERS?
ONLY TWO MAN-EATERS? POOH! I CAN HANDLE A DOZEN AT A TIME!
YAY!
HE'S SO BRAVE!
WE'LL HELP YOU, SAHIB!
I DON'T NEED ANY HELP FROM BUNGLING AMATEURS. JUST KEEP OUT OF MY WAY. THAT'S ALL.
THE SAHIB IS BRAVE AND FEARLESS. ALL THE SAME, TWO MAN-EATERS ARE A BIT TOO MUCH FOR HIM TO HANDLE ON HIS OWN.
YES, WE'LL FOLLOW AND KEEP AN EYE ON HIM.
WE'LL MAKE SURE, HE DOESN'T SPOT US.
WHAT HAVE I LET MYSELF IN FOR THIS TIME? T...T... TWO MAN-EATERS...
YEOW!
SQUEAK!
IT'S ONLY A SQUIRREL! WHAT A NINNY I AM.

THE JUNGLE IS SO QUIET. I BET THERE ARE NO MAN-EATERS AT ALL. THOSE VILLAGERS ARE ONLY IMAGINING THINGS.

4EOW!

RROARR!

HELP! HE'S AFTER ME!

RROWR

MEANWHILE—

NO SIGN OF THE MAN-EATERS. I THINK WE'LL TAKE A BREAK.

GOOD!

L...L... LOOK!

A LEOPARD! THE MAN-EATER!

AND WE HAVE NOTHING TO DEFEND OURSELVES WITH!

W...WHAT'S HE DOING?

HE'S PLAYING CAT AND MOUSE WITH US, THAT'S ALL.

ELSEWHERE—

HE'S STILL AFTER ME!

LOOK! THERE'S THE SAHIB!
THE LEOPARD! HE'S SEEN THE SAHIB TOO!
RROWR!
YEOW!
RROAR!
THUD!
BONK!
SAHIB! SAHIB! YOU'VE GOT THEM BOTH!
DIDN'T I TELL YOU I WOULD! TACKLING TWO MAN-EATERS—EASY AS SNAPPING YOUR FINGERS!

Shikari Shambu
Based on an idea sent by Sanjay Pai, No. 313. 3rd Cross, III Phase, II Block, Banashankari, 3rd Stage, Bangalore 560085.
Illustrations: V B. Halbe
ONE DAY A JEWELLER CAME TO SEE SHAMBU —
SHAMBU, I'M RUINED, UTTERLY RUINED! WHAT SHALL I DO? OH! WHAT SHALL I DO? BOO HOO! BOO HOO!
CALM, DOWN, CALM DOWN. AND TELL ME EVERYTHING.
WELL, I WAS CROSSING THE FOREST WITH A BAG CONTAINING MY JEWELLERY... SUDDENLY I HEARD A ROAR! IT WAS A LEOPARD!
" I FLUNG THE BAG AT THE LEOPARD...
YEOW!
... AND RACED AWAY! "
THUD!
NOW I WANT YOU TO FIND THAT LEOPARD AND GET MY BAG.
I SEE...
I'M PREPARED TO PAY RS.2000.

WHAT ARE WE WAITING FOR? LET'S GO.
BUT... BUT...
THESE ARE THE PUG MARKS OF A LEOPARD!
A LEOP... LEOPARD!
LOOK OUT! THERE HE COMES!
RUN!
ROAR
ROAR!
HELP!
GET DOWN!
KEEP RUNNING! HE'S GAINING.
GET DOWN, YOU COWARD! AND RUN!

DUCK!
HUH! WHAT DUCK? WHERE'S THE DUCK?
CLUNK!
EE!
THUD!
SHAMBU, YOU'VE DONE IT! YOU'VE CAUGHT THE LEOPARD!
HERE. TAKE YOUR BAG.
ALL THE JEWELS ARE HERE. HOW CAN I THANK YOU!
RS.2000 WILL BE THANKS ENOUGH.

Shikari Shambu
Script : Luis M. Fernandes
Illustrations: V B Halbe
SOME JOURNALISTS ARE COMING TO INTERVIEW ME.
MY PICTURE WILL BE IN ALL THE PAPERS TOMORROW!
I'LL BE FAMOUS...! I...!
ALL RIGHT. NOW HAVE YOUR MILK.
TRING! TRING!
THAT MUST BE THEM!
COMING! COMING!
WELCOME!
WHAT A BEAUTIFUL HOUSE YOU HAVE HERE.
SURROUNDED BY NATURE.
I FEEL AT HOME ONLY WHEN I AM AMONG MY FRIENDS, THE ANIMALS.
COME IN AND SEE MY TROPHIES.
COME IN!

A PASSING BEAR DECIDES TO ACCEPT THE INVITATION TOO...
...AND SHUFFLES INSIDE WITH THE OTHERS.
THIS WAY, GENTLEMEN!
I BOUGHT... I MEAN, I BAGGED THIS WILD BUFFALO IN ASSAM.
AND THIS ELEPHANT IN AFRICA...
AND HERE WE HAVE A...
...BEAR!
THAT'S RIGHT, IT'S A BEAR!
YOU SHOULD HAVE BEEN THERE WHEN I WAS WRESTLING WITH HIM.
I CAUGHT HIM BY HIS NECK AND...

...AND...
AND...
B-
BEAR!
AEEEEI
AAAAH!
OOPS
BONK
CLICK!
CLICK
THE NEXT DAY—
YOU WERE RIGHT.
YOU'RE IN ALL
THE PAPERS!
NEWS
Shambu
Captures
Bear!

Shikari Shambu

Based on a story sent by
Ashok Khatri
68, Riverside Road, Indore 452007

Illustrations :
V.B. Halbe

...I WAS SITTING LIKE THIS ON A LOG AND A TIGER CAME AND POUNCED ON ME!
OH, GOD! I HOPE IT DIDN'T KILL YOU, SAHEB!
OH, NO! I CAUGHT IT BY ITS NECK...
...LIKE THIS.
UCCK!
SAHEB! SAHEB! LET ME GO! I'M NOT THE TIGER!
SORRY. SOMETIMES I GET CARRIED AWAY.
ANOTHER TIME I WAS TRACKING IN AMERICA... I MEAN AUSTRALIA AND...
HE MIGHT CATCH MY NECK AGAIN.
I'D BETTER NOT SIT NEXT TO HIM.
...A LION SUDDENLY CAME UP BEHIND ME.

... BUT I SMELT IT AND STRETCHING OUT MY ARM BEHIND ME...
... CAUGHT IT IN A STRANGLEHOLD!
URRGH!
THE LEOPARD!
NOT A LEOPARD, A...
... A LION... AAH!
BONK
I-IT'S OUT COLD. L-LET'S TIE IT UP BEFORE IT COMES ROUND.
OH, IT WAS SO BRAVE OF YOU TO HOLD THE LEOPARD WHILE I KNOCKED IT OUT SAHEB!
OH, THIS IS NOTHING!
I HAVE NEVER SEEN SUCH RAW COURAGE!
ONCE I WAS EXPLORING IN THE ANTARCTIC AND...
OH-OH, MY NECK'S IN DANGER AGAIN.

Shikari Shambu
Script : Luis M. Fernandes
Illustrations: V.B. Halbe
COME ON! COME ON! HURRY!
WHY DOES HE WANT THIS HUGE CAGE?
HE SAYS HE'S GOING TO STET A TIGER!
PUT IT DOWN HERE!
EASY THERE, EASY! DON'T BREAK IT!
YOU CAN GO NOW, BUT COME BACK LATER WITH MORE MEN!
WE'LL HAVE TO CARRY A TIGER!

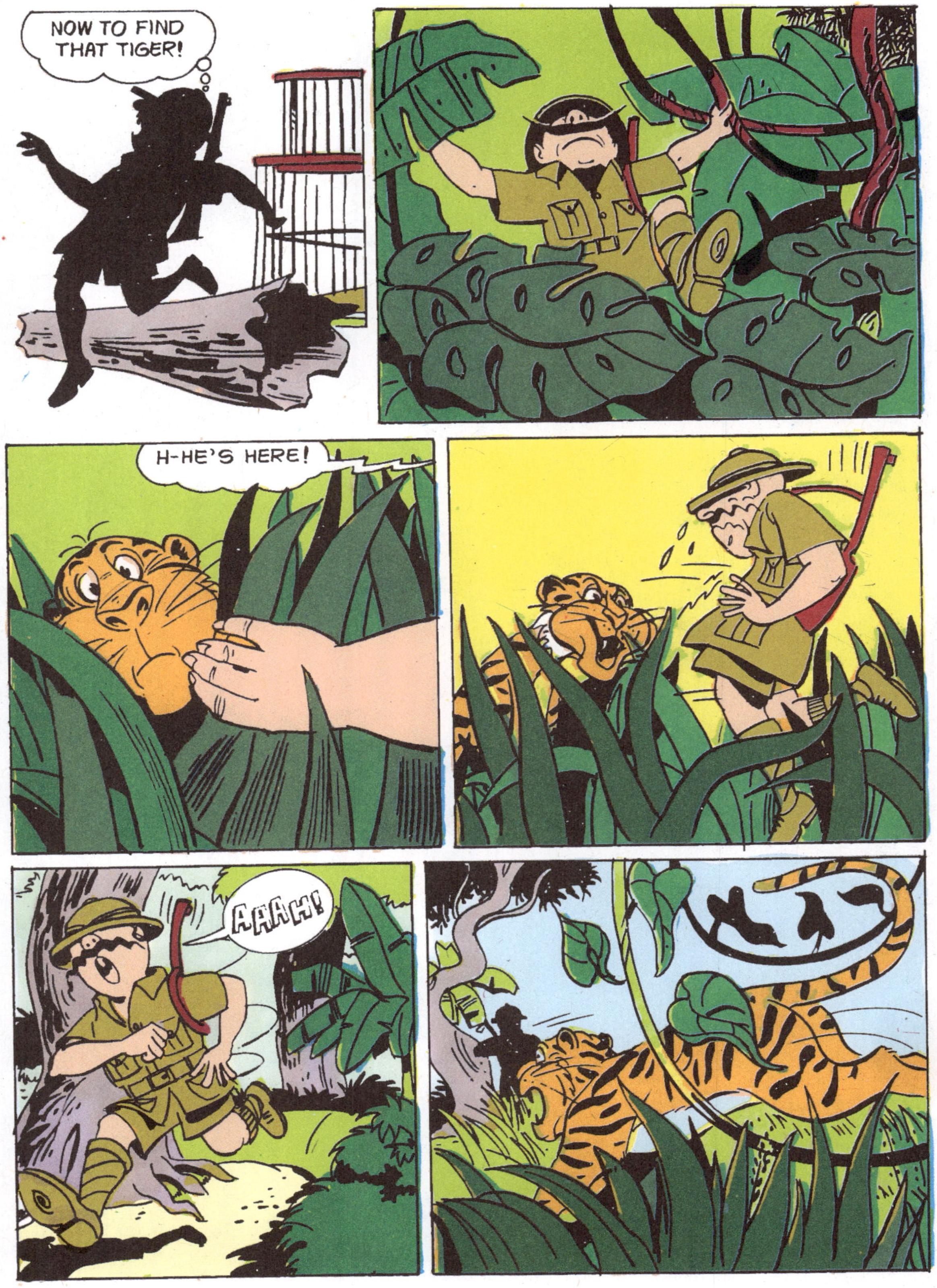
NOW TO FIND THAT TIGER!
H-HE'S HERE!
AAAH!

HELP!
SAHEB HAS STET THE TIGER!
YOU WERE VERY BRAVE, SAHEB.
CAUGHT BY AN AMATEUR — BAH!

Shikari Shambu
Script: Luis M. Ferrandes
Illustrations: V.B. Halbe
... A RONGER HAS TO BE ALERT AT ALL TIMES...
SO KEEP YOUR EYES OPEN!
AHA! ANIMAL TRACKS!
WHERE?
COME ON, WE'LL FOLLOW THE ANIMAL TO ITS LAIR!
ABOUT AN HOUR LATER—
WE ARE GOING AROUND IN CIRCLES!
WHERE ARE THOSE ANIMAL TRACKS ANYWAY?
THERE! THERE!
THOSE! AREN'T THEY YOUR OWN SHOEPRINTS?
SO THEY ARE!

I... ER... WELL...
HERE! THOSE MUST BE ANIMAL TRACKS!
THESE ARE ANIMAL TRACKS! NO MISTAKE ABOUT IT!
WHY, I CAN EVEN GET A FAINT SMELL OF THE CREATURE!
WHAT A TALENT I'VE DISCOVERED IN MYSELF!
HOW MANY RONGER COULD TRACK AN ANIMAL BY SCENT?
I'M UNIQUE! THE GREATEST RONGER IN THE WORLD!
OH, THIS SMELLS LIKE... LIKE...

... AN ELEPHANT!
G-GOOD GOD! AN ELEPHANT!
AAAH!
THAT WAS A NARROW ESCAPE!
WE MUST BE CAREFUL. KEEP YOUR EARS COCKED! LISTEN TO EVERY SOUND...
ROARRRR!
THAT WAS A VERY LOUD SOUND!
Y-YES
YOU'VE USED YOUR EYES, YOUR NOSE AND YOUR EARS. WHAT DO YOU PLAN TO USE NOW?
... MY LEGS! RUN!

Shikari Shambu
Based on a story sent by Sanjay Pai
No. 313, 3rd Cross,
Block
Banashankari, 3rd Stage,
Bangalore 560085
Illustrations: V B. Halbe
THIS JUNGLE IS DANGEROUS! SOME YEARS AGO A SCIENTIFIC EXPEDITION CAME HERE, LIKE US IN SEARCH OF PLANTS. .
...AND NEVER RETURNED
. . (GULP)... I'M GLAD WE HAVE THE BRAVE EXPLORER SHIKARI SHAMBU TO GUIDE US.
ER... SHAMBU, WHAT'S THAT NOISE?
N-NOISE?
OOOOOOO
I... I'LL GO AND SEE.
AAH!
SHAMBU IS RUNNING. SOME FEROCIOUS ANIMAL MUST BE CHASING HIM.
RUN!
WHY ARE THEY RUNNING?

THEY MUST'VE SEEN THE ANIMAL THAT WAS MAKING THAT GHASTLY NOISE!
ZOOM!
I'D BETTER RUN FASTER.
THE BRAVE SHAMBU HAS TAKEN THE LEAD SO AS TO GUIDE US.
CREAK CREAK
CRACK!
HELP!
SPLASH
THERE'S A CROCODILE COMING TOWARDS US!
WE'RE DONE FOR!

SHAMBU! SAVE US!
I... I...
SNAP!
AAH!
DONK!
WHERE AM I? WHO AM I?
SHAMBU HAS DRIVEN AWAY THE CROCODILE! WE'RE SAVED!
PROFESSOR, LOOK!
HE HAS LED US STRAIGHT TO THE PLANTS WE WERE LOOKING FOR!
SHAMBU, YOU'RE THE MOST EXTRAORDINARY MAN I'VE EVER MET.
I DO MY BEST... HEH-HEH

Shikari Shambu

Based on a story sent by Sanjay Pai,
No. 313, 3rd Cross,
III Phase, II Block,
Banashankari, 3rd Stage.
Bangalore 560085.
Illustrations :
V.B. Halbe

ALL RIGHT, FOLKS. TIME TO BOARD THE BUS. COME ON. HURRY UP!
AW... GIVE US SOME MORE TIME.
YES, WE'RE HAVING A LOT OF FUN.
NO ARGUMENTS, PLEASE. WE'VE GOT TO GO A LONG WAY. SO HURRY UP AND START BOARDING THE BUS.
INSIDE THE BUS —
EEEK! LOOK! LOOK AT THAT ANIMAL!
YEOW! LET ME OUT! LET ME OUT!
YEOW! IT'S A... IT'S A... LET'S GET OUT OF HERE!
HELP! HELP!
HELLO, WHAT'S HAPPENING?
HELP! HELP!
WHAT'S THE MATTER?
THERE'S AN ANIMAL INSIDE THE BUS.
OH! HELP US, PLEASE!
HUH! PANICKY FELLOWS! I BET THEY WERE ONLY SCARED BY A MOUSE OR SOMETHING.

THERE IT IS... IT'S A...
YEOW!
HE CAN'T FOLLOW ME UP THIS LADDER...
YEEE! HELP! I'M FALLING!
ZIP! ZIP! ZIP!
THUD!
LOOK AT THAT BRAVE SHIKARI!
WHAT A NOVEL WAY TO CATCH A TIGER!
HE MUST BE SHIKARI SHAMBU. HE'S THE ONLY ONE WHO HUNTS TIGERS IN THIS FASHION!
SMILE. SIR. YOUR PICTURE WILL BE ON THE FRONT PAGE OF EVERY NEWS-PAPER TOMORROW!

Shikari Shambu

Based on a story sent by
Sanjay Pai
No. 313, 3rd Cross,
III Phase, II Block,
Banashankari, 3rd Stage,
Bangalore 560085.

Illustrations:
V. B. Halbe

AND SO—
SEE THAT FELLOW THERE? THAT'S THE FAMOUS SHIKARI SHAMBU.
THANK HEAVENS HE'S HERE! I'LL SLEEP SOUNDLY IN OUR TENT TONIGHT.
WHAT WITH THE MAN-EATER PROWLING ABOUT, I HAVEN'T SLEPT A WINK FOR A WHOLE WEEK.
YES, BUT SEE THAT YOU DON'T KEEP ME AWAKE WITH YOUR SNORING.
HEY, YOU TWO! ARE YOU GOING INTO THE JUNGLE?
YES, TO CHOP WOOD.
I'M COMING ALONG.
YOU NEED A STRONG MAN TO PROTECT YOU.
IN THE JUNGLE—
I HOPE THE MAN-EATER ISN'T AROUND.
WHAT'S THE MATTER? YOU'RE TREMBLING.
HEH HEH! NOTHING. JUST A TOUCH OF FEVER, THAT'S ALL.
ROAR
EIIEEE!

RUN! RUN!
QUICK. LET'S SHIN UP A TREE.
WE'RE LUCKY. THE TIGER'S CHOSEN SHAMBU FOR HIS DINNER.
EEEAGH!
ZING!
THUD!
HEY, THE TIGER'S OUT COLD.
WHAT A STUNT! ONLY SHIKARI SHAMBU COULD'VE WORKED IT OUT.
LATER-
YOU SHOULD'VE SEEN HIM TACKLING THE MAN-EATER, SAHIB. THE MAN WAS BURNING WITH FEVER AND YET...
...HE CAUGHT IT... AS EASILY AS TAKING COINS FROM A BABY.
SHAMBU, LET ME CONGRATULATE YOU...
AND MY... HEH HEH!
YOUR BONUS ...HERE IT IS. HEAVEN ALONE KNOWS, YOU'VE EARNED IT.

Shikari Shambu
Script : Luis M Fernandes
Illustrations: V.B. Halbe
I'VE BEEN ASKED TO TRACK DOWN A DANGEROUS LEOPARD...
... A MAN-EATER!
MAKE SURE YOU'RE BACK BY TEA-TIME!
MOTHER IS ARRIVING TODAY AND WE HAVE TO MEET HER AT THE BUS-STOP AT 5 O' CLOCK!
DOES SHE EXPECT ME TO DROP EVERYTHING AND RUSH TO THE BUS-STOP AT 5 O'CLOCK ?!
ONCE WE RONGERS ARE ON THE TRAIL OF AN ANIMAL WE LOSE ALL SENSE OF TIME!
I WON'T RETURN TILL I'VE BAGGED THAT LEOPARD!
AH, HERE'S MY MACHAN.

32

SPLASH
NOW I'M IN BIGGER TROUBLE... I'M HEADING STRAIGHT FOR THE WATERFALL!
EEEE-YOW!
KER-SPLOSH
THANK HEAVENS, I'M STILL IN ONE PIECE...
FOR A MOMENT, I THOUGHT...
SO THERE YOU ARE!
WHY ARE YOU SO LATE?! GET OUT OF THAT WATER QUICKLY!
!
THE BUS IS HERE! COME ON!
SOMEHOW SHE ALWAYS HAS HER WAY.

Shikari Shambu

Script : Dev Nadkarni

Illustrations : V. B. Halbe

RUN!
FASTER... HE HAS A GUN.
O GOD! HIS TAIL TALKS TOO.
N... NEVER HAVE I... S... SEEN SUCH A TIGER.
I... I'LL SIGHT HIM FROM THE TOP OF THIS HILL.

CRASH
Y-YOU TWO WERE IN THAT COSTUME!
Y— YES.
I'D HAVE KNOCKED YOU DOWN YOU KNOW.
TH... THANK GOD YOU DIDN'T!
BUT WAIT A MINUTE... FE FI FO FUM... I STILL SMELL A TIGER.
T... TIGER BEHIND Y... YOU.
GROWL

Shikari Shambu
Based on a story sent by Sanjay Pai
No 313, 3rd Cross, ill Phase, II Block,.
Banashankari, 3rd Stage, Bangalore 560085
Illustrations: V B.Halbe
IT'S SO GOOD TO COME TO A PLACE WHERE ALL THE ANIMALS ARE BEHIND BARS...
...WHERE THEY CAN'T DO YOU ANY HARM... HEH-HEH.
ER...UNCLE, DON'T THEY HAVE A RHINOCEROS HERE?
A RHINOCEROS? OF COURSE THEY HAVE ONE... COME THIS WAY.
THERE IT IS!
DOESN'T IT LOOK FEROCIOUS?
YES, WHAT IF IT WERE TO ESCAPE?
E-ESCAPE?
I DON'T THINK IT COULD ESCAPE FROM THERE...
AAAH!

THE RHINOCEROS IS BREAKING OUT!

WHAT SHOULD WE DO, UNCLE...

UNCLE, WHERE ARE YOU?

I'LL BE SAFE HERE... I HOPE.

IT'S BECOME SO QUIET SUDDENLY. I WONDER WHAT'S GOING ON.

CAN'T SEE THE RHINO ANYWHERE. PERHAPS HE... HE...!

AAH!

HELP!

TR-AACCK!
SLAM!
UNCLE, UNCLE ARE YOU ALL RIGHT?
MR. SHAMBU, YOU! I SHOULD'VE KNOWN!
I...I...
ONLY THE GREAT SHIKARI SHAMBU COULD HAVE HANDLED THAT RHINOCEROS AS DEFTLY AS YOU DID!
OH, IT WAS NOTHING, MR. SUPERINTENDENT. WHY, ONCE WHEN I WAS IN KENYA...
SIR!
ANOTHER PORTION OF THE WALL HAS COLLAPSED!
WHAT!
MR. SHAMBU, I HOPE YOU WILL STAY TO HELP US...
SORRY I HAVE TO RUSH!
CALLED AWAY ON ANOTHER EMERGENCY PERHAPS! OH, HE HAS A WAY WITH ANIMALS, THAT MAN!

Shikari Shambu
Script : Dev Nadkarni
Illustrations: V.B. Halbe
QUICK, PACK UP MY KIT. "SAFARI" MAGAZINE HAS ASSIGNED ME A NEW JOB.
WHAT KIND?
TO SHOOT TIGERS!
GOOD LORD! WHY WOULD THEY WANT YOU TO DO THAT?
OH! YOU'LL NEVER UNDERSTAND SUCH COMPLEX THINGS.
!
LATER—
LET'S FIND A GOOD SPOT AND BEGIN OUR JOB.
YES.
THIS PLACE SEEMS FINE...
WE'LL SETTLE DOWN HERE AND WAIT FOR A TIGER.
RUSTLE RUSTLE
HUSH! SOMEONE'S COMING.
OH! IT'S A BEAR.
SO WHAT? LET'S TRY IT OUT ON THIS BEAR FIRST... READY ... AIM... SHOOT!
CLICK

AH, WHAT A PICTURE THAT'LL MAKE!
BUT WHAT WE WANT IS TIGERS!
OH, FOR A TIGER!
LATE IN THE EVENING—
WHAT ROTTEN LUCK... NOT A TIGER THE WHOLE DAY...
PATIENCE, PATIENCE!
IT'S GETTING DARKER... I'LL FIX MY FLASH...
HEY!
WHAT IS IT?
A TIGER'S TRACKS! HE MUST BE SOMEWHERE AROUND.
LET'S KNEEL BEHIND THAT BUSH WITH OUR CAMERA READY.
YES... LET'S.
HOW SOFT THE GROUND IS... LOOKS LIKE SOMEONE'S LEFT CUSHIONS HERE...
FANCY SOMEBODY LEAVING CUSHIONS IN THIS JUNGLE!
...AND A FUNNY DESIGN TOO — YELLOW WITH BLACK STRIPES.
?

YELLOW... BLACK... STRIPES!! WHAAAA...
?
EEEAAAH
GROWL!
SHOOT, SH...SHOOT.
CLICK!
FLASH!
!
WAIT, WAIT...COME BACK HERE!
CLICK!
STOP, YOU COWARD! OUR PHOTO-SESSION HAS JUST BEGUN.
WHAT A PICTURE THAT'LL BE!

Shikari Shambu
Script: Iyer Prasad B.
Illustrations: V.B Halbe
SHAMBU. WE WANT TO KNOW HOW FAST A CHEETAH CAN RUN...
...SO WE WANT YOU TO HELP US.
WE'VE MEASURED THE CLEARING FROM THIS LINE ONWARDS — IT'S A HUNDRED METRES.
WE HAVE TO MAKE A CHEETAH SPRINT ACROSS THIS DISTANCE AND WORK OUT THE TIME IT TAKES.
HMMM...
WE'LL THEN KNOW HOW FAST IT RUNS.
I'LL RUSTLE UP SOME BEATERS TOMORROW.
EXCELLENT!
THE NEXT DAY —
YOU STAY HERE. I'LL GO WITH THE BEATERS AND SEE IF I CAN FIND A CHEETAH.
GREAT!
IN THE FOREST —
ALL RIGHT, FAN OUT EVERYBODY AND MAKE AS LOUD A NOISE AS YOU CAN.

WOW! WHAT A DIN THEY'RE MAKING!
THUM PIT
THURMPITY! THUMP! THUMP!
BUMP
I'LL GO AHEAD OF THE BEATERS. THEY SURE ARE SCARING A LOT OF ANIMALS.
BUMPITY! BUMPITY!
?
MEANWHILE—
I'LL CLIMB UP THIS TREE AND SEE IF ANY CHEETAHS ARE AROUND.
THUMPITY! THUMPITY!
YEEE! A WILD BUFFALO!

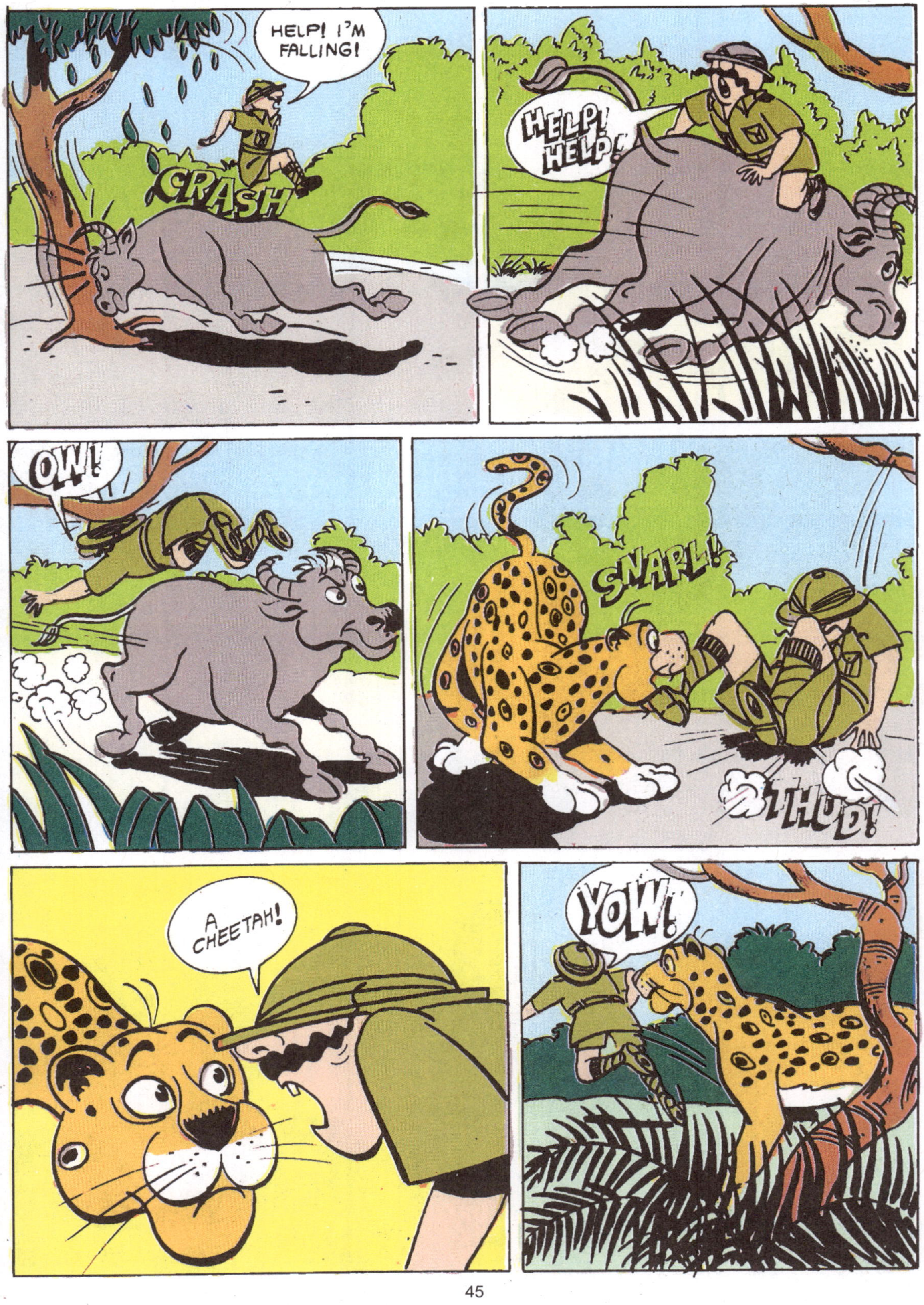
HELP! I'M FALLING!
CRASH
HELP! HELP!
OW!
SNARL!
THUD!
A CHEETAH!
YOW!

GROWL!
MEANWHILE—
THE BEATERS ARE COMING CLOSE.
THUMP
HUMP
LOOK! HERE COMES SHAMBU.
THERE'S SOMETHING AFTER HIM!
IT'S A CHEETAH!
JUST LOOK AT SHAMBU RUN!
I THOUGHT THE CHEETAH WAS THE FASTEST ANIMAL, BUT HERE'S SHAMBU BEATING ONE HANDS DOWN.

Shikari Shambu

Script : Prasad Iyer

Illustrations: V B. Halbe

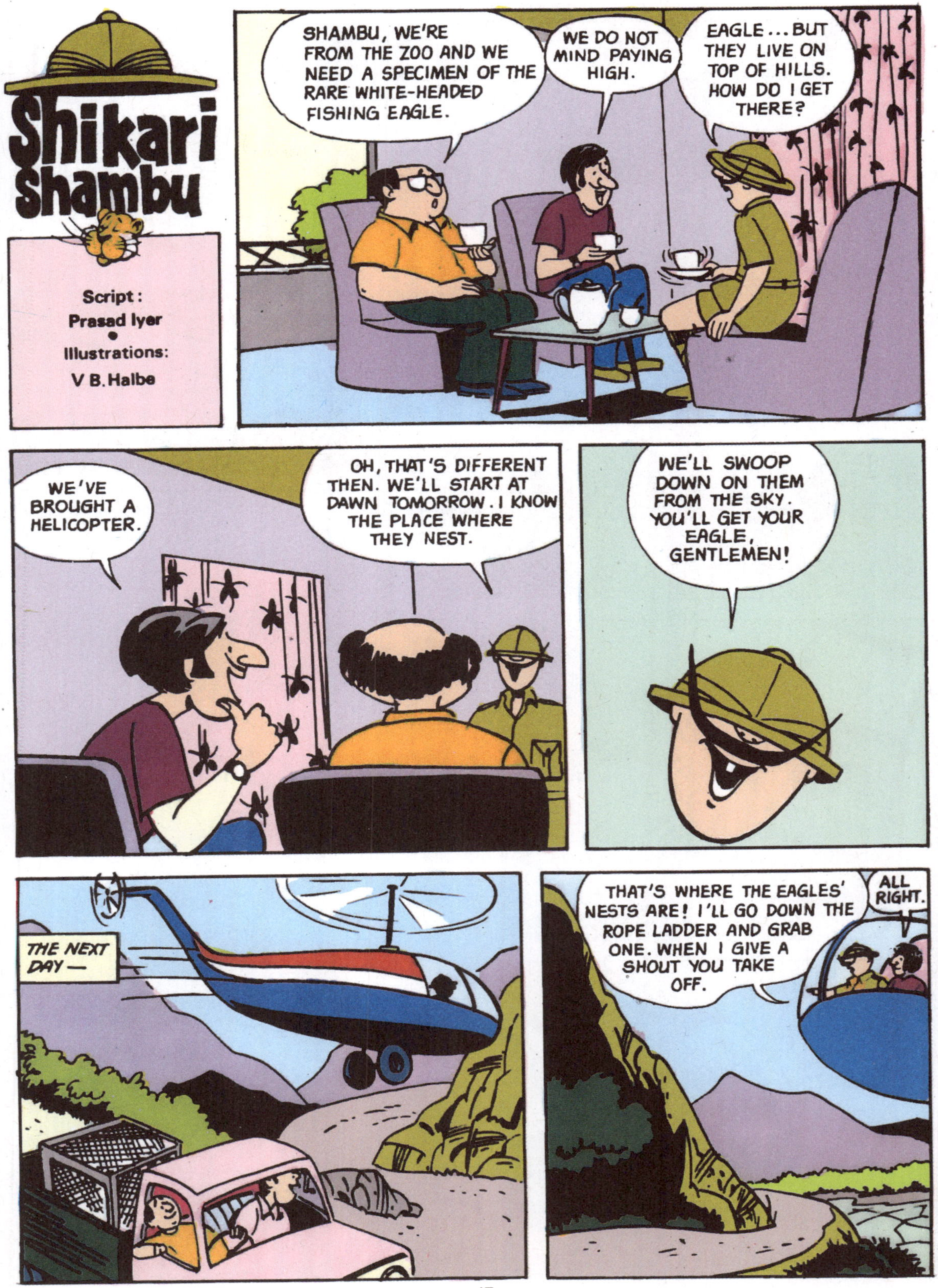

HEH HEH! IT'LL BE EASY TO CATCH AN EAGLE. THEY'RE SO STUPID.
HERE'S ONE.
EEEYOW!
HEY!
THE SIGNAL! SHAMBU'S GOT THE EAGLE. TIME I TOOK OFF!

ZOOM!
YAAAAH!
TWANG!
WHAT A BEAUTIFUL SPECIMEN!
CONGRATULATIONS, SHAMBU. I'VE NEVER SEEN AN EAGLE CAUGHT THIS WAY BEFORE.

Shikari Shambu

Script: Iyer Prasad B.

Illustrations : V.B. Halbe

SOON —
What have you brought?
This shikari, O great chief.
Good! Untie him. Let the warriors' dance begin.
YEEAH!
YEEAH!
SUDDENLY —
BANG!
SNICK!
RROAR
I'LL MAKE FOR THE PALISADE.
Run! Run!
Help! Help! He's after me!
RROAR!

GROWL!
EEIEE!
ZIP!
YEE!
RROAR
HEY, LOOK! IT'S SHAMBU. WHAT'S THAT HE'S WEARING?
HEY, SHAMBU! OVER HERE!
WHAT'S THAT ON YOUR HEAD, SHAMBU?
EH?
OH! IT'S THE HEADDRESS YOU WANTED. I THOUGHT I'D GET IT FOR YOU AFTER ALL.

Shikari Shambu
This story has won a consolation prize in the Shikari Shambu story-writing contest.
Story by: Umesh Pande
317, M.G. Road, Malnargunj, Indore-452 002 (M.P.)
Illustrations: V.B. Halbe
ONE DAY SHIKARI SHAMBU WAS DOZING IN THE WARM WINTER SUN.
ZZZ
SHAMBU SAHIB!
SHIKARI SHAMBU! COME QUICKLY.
WHAT'S THE MATTER?
A MANEATING TIGER IS ON THE PROWL NEAR BY.
WHERE IS HE GOING?
TO GET HIS GUN, I THINK.
...WITH AN EXPERT HUNTER LIKE HIM AROUND, WHAT HAVE WE TO FEAR!
YES, YES, OF COURSE. YOU'RE QUITE SAFE WITH ME AROUND.
HERE'S YOUR RIFLE.

54

Panel 1: "WE'VE ARRANGED FOR A JEEP AND A CAGE. WE ARE SURE YOU'LL CATCH HIM AS SOON AS YOU SEE HIM."

Panel 2: "WHY DON'T YOU GET INTO THE JEEP?" "NO, NO! WE DON'T WANT TO BE A DISTRACTION."

Panel 3: "WE'LL FOLLOW YOU WITH THE CAGE IN THIS VAN." "UHH! ALL RIGHT."

Panel 4: "MY LUCKY DAY. FIVE DELICIOUS HUMANS!"

Panel 5: "I'LL HIDE IN THE BUSHES BELOW."

Panel 7: "OOH! HELP!"

WHAT HAPPENED?
I CAN'T SEE SHIKARI SHAMBU IN THE JEEP.
UNGUIDED, THE JEEP VEERED OFF THE TRACK...
... AND HIT ONE OF THE BUSHES.
AS LUCK WOULD HAVE IT, IT WAS THE VERY BUSH WHERE THE TIGER WAS LURKING IN WAIT.
CRASH
HE HAS DONE IT AGAIN!
LONG LIVE SHIKARI SHAMBU!
WAH! SHIKARI SHAMBU! YOU CAUGHT THE TIGER WITHOUT FIRING A SINGLE SHOT!
HE MUST HAVE FAINTED AT THE VERY SIGHT OF SHAMBU SAHEB. HA HA!
HEE HEE!

Shikari Shambu
This story has won a consolation prize in the Shikari Shambu story-writing contest.
Story by: Mahesh Jotwani
Baba Garib Das Marg, Sindhi Camp, Kacchi Kholi, Akola-444 001.
Illustrations: V.B. Halbe
IT WAS A WARM SUMMER'S DAY—
GREAT WEATHER FOR FISHING.
JUST AS HE REACHED THE RIVER-SIDE —
SHIKARI SHAMBU, THERE'S A LEOPARD AROUND...
A MAN-EATER!
YOU MUST CATCH HIM.
I WILL IF I MEET HIM. BUT TODAY I'M GOING TO FISH.
IT WAS A LONG, LONG WAIT.
YAWN
SUDDENLY THERE WAS A DOWNWARD JERK ON THE LINE.
SHIKARI SHAMBU PULLED BACK WITH ALL HIS MIGHT.
YANK

THE TUG-OF-WAR WENT ON FOR A WHILE —
IT MUST BE A REAL BIG FISH TO PULL LIKE THIS.
THE LEOPARD WAS ABOUT TO POUNCE ON SHIKARI SHAMBU WHEN —
GOT IT!
TONK
WHAT WAS THAT? OH, GOSH!
THAT EVENING —
SHIKARI SHAMBU, HERE'S YOUR REWARD FOR CAPTURING THE LEOPARD!
WHAT QUICK WORK!
AND WHAT A GREAT FISH! BIG ENOUGH TO TREAT US ALL TO A FEAST OF FISH CURRY.

TINKLE

The Best Collections of Stories of Suppandi, Shambu and Tantri are worth their weight in Gold!

Tinkle Collection—where every comic is individually dedicated to your favourite Tinkle characters!

To buy Tinkle collection, visit your nearest bookstore or buy online at www.amarchitrakatha.com or call 022-40497417/31/35/36

Shikari Shambu
Script: Denis
Illustrations: V.B. Halbe
IT'S TIME I TOOK A HOLIDAY.
HOLIDAY? I SUPPOSE YOU MUST BE AWFULLY TIRED DOING NOTHING...
MAMA, I THINK SHAMBU IS RIGHT. WE ALL DESERVE A HOLIDAY.
YOU'RE RIGHT. I AM BEGINNING TO GET BORED.
WE START FOR THE HILL-STATION IN THE EVENING.
STOP BEHAVING LIKE AN EXCITED SCHOOLBOY, SHAMBU.
LATER—
YOUR MOTHER WAS RATHER UPSET WITH ME TODAY.
ACTUALLY SHE QUITE LIKES YOU, SHAMBU.
SOON—
WHERE ARE YOU GOING, SHAMBU?
FOR A HOLIDAY— TO THE HILL-STATION.
YOU'RE TAKING A BIG RISK, SHAMBU. A MAN-EATER IS ON THE RAMPAGE OUT THERE.

ER...ER...I...I THINK WE SHOULD POSTPONE THIS TRIP. FO...FOR YOUR SAFETY.
NO!
RIFLE... WHERE'S MY RIFLE?
IT'S ON THE CARRIER.
DON'T WASTE TIME, SHAMBU. DRIVE ON.
RUINED! MY HOLIDAY IS RUINED.
AFTER A COUPLE OF HOURS —
CAN'T THIS JEEP GO ANY FASTER?
EH...
EVERYONE'S OVERTAKING US!
SPLUTTER
SPLUTTER
I'LL GO AND CHECK THE ENGINE.
OH!
DON'T WORRY, LADIES. I'LL FIX IT IN A MOMENT.

TIGER!
ROAR... ROAR...
OH...
RR...ROAR
I'LL HELP YOU.
ROAR... ROAR...
SNAP
SHAMBU IS SAFE. THANK YOU!
WHO IS SHE?
THIS LADY IS AS BRAVE AS SHIKARI SHAMBU!
FRIENDS— MEET MY MOTHER-IN-LAW!
WELL DONE, MADAM!

Shikari Shambu

Based on a story sent by Sanjay Pai, Bangalore

Illustrations :
V.B. Halbe

LET'S PARK THE VAN HERE.
SUDDENLY-
HELP! HELP! TIGER!
WHAT THE...
RUN! RUN!
IT'S THE MANEATER!
LOOK! THERE HE COMES!
RUN!
I'LL MAKE FOR THE VAN AND ESCAPE...
SLAM
SHAMBU IS MAKING A GETAWAY. HE'S LEAVING US IN THE LURCH.

IT IS IN REVERSE GEAR. AND THE GEAR IS STUCK.
...AND NOW THE ACCELERATOR IS STUCK!
START THE CAMERA! WHAT A SCENE!
I CAN'T STOP! THE BRAKE'S JAMMED.
THUD!
THE TIGER IS TRAPPED!
AND WE'VE FILMED IT ALL!
WELL DONE, SHAMBU!
WELL DONE, SAHIB!

Shikari Shambu
This story won a consolation prize in the Shikari Shambu story-writing competition
Story by Master P. Ajay Ghosh
P.O. Dasarahalli BANGALORE-560 057
Illustrations: V.B. Halbe
SHAMBU HAD RECEIVED A MOTORCYCLE AS A GIFT FROM AN ADMIRER—
ISN'T IT A DANDY VEHICLE!
OH, YES! BUT...
... DON'T RIDE IT!
EH?
TWO WHEELERS ARE DANGEROUS!
WHAT NONSENSE!
SEE YOU LATER!
NOOOO! DON'T GO!
WROOOM!

AND SOON—
WHEEEE! THIS IS FUN!
DACOITS! ...EEEEEE!
CAN'T YOU SEE WHERE YOU'RE GOING!
I'LL TEACH YOU A LESSON!
OH NO! NOW THE BRAKES OF MY BIKE ARE GONE.
SNAP
HEY, WHAT ARE YOU DOING? STOP IT! LISTEN...

OFF YOU GO!
HELP!
WROOM
THERE'S NO WAY I CAN STOP!
WHAM
EH?
HEY, NO HITCH-HIKERS
OUR BEAR!

OUR BEAR HAS BEEN FOUND.
MR. SHAMBU IS BRINGING OUR BEAR BACK.
LOOKS LIKE I'VE BECOME A HERO!
CRASH!
CONGRATULATIONS, MR. SHAMBU. WE ARE GREATLY OBLIGED TO YOU FOR BRINGING BACK OUR BEAR. HE HAD WANDERED AWAY AND WE THOUGHT WE WOULD NEVER SEE HIM AGAIN.
HOW CAN I EVER REWARD YOU?
JUST PROVIDE ME TRANSPORT TO GO HOME.
AND SO—
THIS IS BETTER THAN ANY TWO-WHEELER.
WHEE!

Shikari Shambu
This story won a consolation prize in the Shikari Shambu story-writing contest.
Story by: Dhiraj Piparaiya
26 Shirin, Colaba, BOMBAY-400 005
Illustrations : V.B. Halbe
ONE DAY TWO MUSEUM OFFICIALS CAME TO SHAMBU WITH A REQUEST.
A FOREIGN MAGAZINE IS OFFERING A PRIZE OF TWO LAKHS OF RUPEES FOR A PICTURE OF THE YETI.
WE WANT YOU TO LEAD AN UNOFFICIAL EXPEDITION TO THE HIMALAYAS TO GET SOME PICTURES OF THE YETI.
YET...YET... YETI, THE ABOMINABLE SNOWMAN?
UH! OKAY, BUT I'LL HAVE TO BRING ALONG AN ASSISTANT.
FINE! WE LEAVE AS SOON AS WE CAN.
AND, MR. SHAMBU, YOUR SHARE WILL BE RS.25,000 IF WE SUCCEED.
A FEW DAYS LATER THE EXPEDITION WAS TREKKING THROUGH THE HIMALAYAS.
MR SHAMBU, WITH YOU IN CHARGE, THE EXPEDITION JUST CAN'T FAIL!
YOU WILL GET YOUR PHOTOGRAPHS. JUST KEEP YOUR CAMERAS HANDY!
WE WILL SET UP OUR CAMP HERE.
YOU DO THAT! WE'LL GO AND LOOK FOR THE YETI!
I'VE HEARD THAT YETIS ARE ELUSIVE CREATURES.
OH, WE'LL FIND HIM ALL RIGHT.
FIND HIM! HOW?
I'VE GOT A BAIT INSIDE THIS BAG! HEE! HEE!

JUST PUT ON THIS COSTUME. PERHAPS THE YETI MAY SEE IT AND COME TO CATCH YOU.
UH.....OKAY. I'LL GO INTO THAT CAVE AND CHANGE!
YOU WAIT HERE!
DON'T TAKE LONG!
MINUTES LATER-
AAAAAH!
!?!
TH... THE YETI!!
OOH!
AAAAAAAH!

71

AND IT'S ALL DUE TO MR. SNOWBALL... ER... I MEAN MR. SHAMBU HERE.
LETS TAKE THE ROLL OUT OF THE CAMERA. WE MUST HAVE THE FILM DEVELOPED AS QUICKLY AS POSSIBLE.
OH NO! I FORGOT TO PUT THE FILM IN THE CAMERA!
WHAT!
WELL, IT'S NOT MY FAULT IF YOU TWO CLOWNS FAILED TO PUT FILM IN THE CAMERA. NOW WE'LL HAVE TO RETURN HOME BECAUSE WE HAVE NO MORE SUPPLIES.
BOO HOO! WE'RE RUINED! WE HAD PUT ALL OUR SAV-INGS INTO THIS SCHEME! BOO HOO!
A FEW DAYS LATER–
OH, HELLO, MR. SHAMBU, WHAT'S NEW?
THIS!
MONEY! BUT HOW DID YOU GET IT?
WELL, YOU GOT SOME TERRIFIC PICTURES OF THE AVALANCHE WITH YOUR CINE CAMERA!
SO I WAS ABLE TO SELL THE PICTURES TO A FILM PRODUCER WHO WANTED TO FILM AN AVALANCHE SCENE FOR TWO LAKHS OF RUPEES!
YIPPEE! WE'RE SAVED!
THREE CHEERS FOR SHIKARI SHAMBU! HIP HIP HURRAY!